Anton the Goatherd

by Alois Carigiet

New York　　　Henry Z. Walck, Incorporated　　　1966

I dedicate this book to all children, both far and near, but especially to my dear friends, the little goatherds of the Surselva—who have tended their goats on craggy mountains, in sunshine and wind and storm, and who know both the joy and the sorrow of a goatherd's life.

I was lucky enough to spend my own childhood in a mountain village, and in my memory the goatherd's horn still wakes me from sleep to start the day.

My main purpose and dearest wish is that this book should bring all my readers the same joy I feel whenever, wandering alone in the mountains of my homeland, I hear the far-off tinkle of a goat's bell.

Flutginas, in spring 1965

Zack, Zick and Zock are three nanny goats who live in a small village high up in the mountains. They belong to Stina, an old woman who lives alone in a little cottage near the village square—except in summer, when Anton lives with her. Anton is a goatherd; he herds all the village goats and takes them up to the meadows every morning. Zack, Zick and Zock are his three favorites. Zack is as white as snow and has no horns. She is sometimes headstrong, which worries Anton. Zick is ruby-red and has only one horn, and Zock is the smallest goat in the whole flock. Anton is especially fond of her and has hung a pretty little bell around her neck. It has a clear tone, and you can hear it from a distance:

Klingelingeling, klingelingeling

Zack, Zick and Zock go everywhere together. Stina opens their stall to let them out so that they can go off to the meadows with Anton. "Anton," calls Stina, "take special care of Zack, Zick and Zock—you know what they are like!" But Anton, standing at the village fountain, listens with only half an ear—and so we come to our story.

Anton blows his horn, which echoes loudly across the village square. The goats come tripping from all the little lanes and alleys. They drink a sip of water at the fountain and then they shake their bells impatiently. The church clock strikes seven, the rooster crows on the fence, the hen cackles, and Fipsi the dog barks loudly. Anton stands at the fountain, calling the roll of the goats:

"Four from old Martina,
Seven from Uncle Paul,
The piebald from Aunt Celina,
The red from the lower stall;
There's Snowy and Brownie, there's Stripy and Spot,
There's one with a black face and one with a dot,
There's red Andrew's four,
And from Marie two more,
And finally here are the best of the flock,
Old Stina's three goats—snow-white Zack, Zick and Zock."

After counting his goats, Anton leads them out of the village. Soon they pass the last pine trees and larches. A white blanket of snow glitters from the mountain peaks, as the goats climb the steep crags.

Now they are up on the highest crag. Anton and Fipsi stretch out on the soft grass and relax. Anton eats his bread and butter and Fipsi chews his sausage, as the warm summer breeze fans their faces. A helicopter flies noisily overhead, and with a cry of kri, kri, kri three crows drive away an eagle. The sun burns in the hazy sky and the fleecy clouds chase each other. Anton tells Fipsi about the wind and the rain that the mountain will soon be sending down.

In a little while it is time for Anton to call the goats together. From the high crag he looks for his flock. Are they all here?

> "Four from old Martina,
>   Seven from Uncle Paul,
>   The piebald from Aunt Celina,
>   The red from the lower stall;
>   There's Snowy and Brownie, there's Stripy and Spot,
>   There's one with a black face and one with a dot,
>   There's red Andrew's four,
>   And from Marie two more,
>   And finally here are the best of the flock,
>   Old Stina's three goats – – – "

Anton calls them all again, but the count is the same. He swallows hard—but he can't see Zack, nor Zick and Zock. All three have disappeared, as if the mountain has swallowed them up. A chill wind has arisen and it whips around Anton's ears. He jumps down from the crag. "Fipsi," he calls. "Come on. We have to find Zack, Zick and Zock. You stay right here," he tells the other goats.

The first raindrops have already fallen, so Anton flings his green jacket around his shoulders and picks up his stick. Then he and Fipsi run as fast as their legs will carry them to the nearest hut, in case Tumasch the dairyman has seen the three strays. Now the heavens open and thunder rolls across the mountains. Anton isn't frightened. He is only a boy, but he can't feel afraid of lightning that looks like the flashing taillight of a car or thunder that sounds like the crash of a church organ. He has only one worry: where are Zack, Zick and Zock?

Now he reaches the hut. The rain streams down as if it is being poured from a bucket. Tumasch, who is an old friend, opens the door right away. "What are you doing out in this weather? Come in and warm yourself by the fire." But Anton has no time.

He asks if Tumasch has seen three goats—a white one, a red one and a tiny one. No, Tumasch hasn't seen any goats. Anton goes straight back through the forest. A tree has been blown down but he doesn't see any goats. Just once he hears the soft tinkle of a little bell, a clear klinge-lingeling, but it seems to come from the other side of the swift-flowing stream. . . . And Anton knows how the wind plays tricks with sounds in the forest.

There are seven claps of thunder, and then no sound but the rain. Anton stands in the middle of the forest. He shouts, and then listens carefully.

He hears a woodpecker pecking on a tree; a blue jay flies past, a squirrel scolds, and a fox slinks along. A whole family of deer stands under a tree, staring curiously at Anton. But today he has no eyes for his friends; he can think only of Zack, Zick and Zock. Whatever will Stina say when he comes home without her goats?

Anton is miserable; sadly he listens to his own voice resounding through the forest. "Come here, Zack, come, Zick . . . come on, Zock." He calls in vain—all he can hear is his cry echoing through the trees.

At last Anton and Fipsi reach the swift stream. There is more water in it than usual because of the storm, and they cannot see the bridge anywhere. But Anton can hear the soft tinkle of a goat bell among the rocks on the other side. It must be Zock who is calling him. How can he cross the stream? Can he jump? But the stream is wide and a jump might be dangerous. Over there, where two rocks are close together . . . he might just be able to get across.

Anton paces up and down for a long time. He can't make up his mind. Then he hears the soft tinkle of the bell again. He measures the distance with his eye once more, stands on the very edge—and jumps.

Anton gets across, but the jump was dangerous; he knows that now. His foot slipped as he jumped and he has sprained his ankle. He takes a step but has to sit down because his ankle hurts. Anton takes off his shoe and stocking and looks at his sore ankle. He plucks a healing herb, washes his foot in a rock pool, and bandages his ankle with a handkerchief. He can't get his shoe back on, so he hangs it around his neck. He picks up his stick and calls his dog. "Come on, Fipsi, we must go."

The path between the rocks is dangerous and Anton grips his stick tightly. Now he is really frightened. Should he go on searching? Then the soft tinkle of the bell sounds a little nearer. Anton presses on, through briers and brambles, over sticks and stones. He crawls through the undergrowth on his hands and knees. At last he reaches the overhanging cliff, stands up, and scans the rocky ground. "Zack! Zick! Zock!"

There are Zack and Zick, lying peacefully in the grass. Their bells hang quiet and still around their necks. Only little Zock stands by the cliff, licking the salty rocks. Her bell swings to and fro. That is the sound Anton heard from so far away.

Anton is delighted. Even though he has hurt his ankle, he has found his goats. But he still has one problem: how to get home before dark. He leads Zack by her bell strap and sets off. They have to get back across the stream. Anton cannot jump over the water because of his sprained ankle. But in the ravine he sees a tree trunk, struck down in a long-ago storm, which has fallen across the stream. This will have to be the bridge they need. Anton leads Zack carefully across the tree trunk. Fipsi has run on ahead and is already on the other side. Zick and Zock follow bravely behind. Now they go back to the meadow and over the crag to where the rest of the flock is waiting impatiently. And they all go home together.

The summer day is nearly over and it is already dark in the village square. Some of the villagers have come out of their houses to find out what has happened to Anton and his flock. Then they hear the goats coming. As always, in front come Zack, Zick and Zock. None of the villagers know what a chase these three have led Anton today.

"Oh look—Anton is limping. Did he fall? What's happened to him? Is he hurt?" the villagers ask each other. No one really knows what has happened, and Anton only smiles and waves his hand cheerfully.

Despite his sore ankle, Anton helps Stina settle the three goats. She lights the way with a lantern, and Zack, Zick and Zock trip into their stall. Anton spreads a handful of dry grass in their trough, and Stina milks them. Then they both leave the stall and close the door.

"Come on, Anton," says Stina. "Let's go inside. Your meal is on the table, and when you have eaten I will see what I can do for your bad ankle."

Anton sits happily at his place in the cozy kitchen. He is hungry because he hasn't had time to eat since noon. Now the cornbread and milk taste twice as good as usual.

When he has finished eating, he tells Stina all about his adventures: about the storm, the forest and the stream; and how he first lost and then found Zack, Zick and Zock. "I told you those three might cause trouble," says Stina. Then she washes his sprained ankle. She gets a little jar of herb salve from a trunk, spreads the salve on a bandage, and wraps it around the ankle. She murmurs a special rhyme:

> "Sun and rain and wind and snow,
> Until the morning do not blow;
> And with the early morning dew
> Make Anton's foot as good as new."

Stina puts out the light. "Good night, Anton." "Good night, Stina." They go off to their own rooms.

The little room where Anton sleeps has gaily flowered wallpaper. His bed is brightly painted, and on the wall hangs a picture of Ursli and Florina. Fipsi sleeps in a basket under the bed. Anton gets undressed and crawls under the covers. Sleep is a long time in coming but then Anton has a marvelous dream; his room becomes as bright as day, and around his bed stand all the forest animals. At the head of the bed are the crows and the eagle from the mountain, and at the foot stands a blue jay, a woodpecker and a squirrel. Just outside the open window are the deer family and the helicopter. The fox is there, too, and a weasel, and Zack, Zick and Zock stand in the middle of the room.

All the animals wish Anton good night. Zack says, "Sleep well, Anton." Zick bleats, "Sweet dreams." But Zock stammers, "Anton, I promise you we will never run away again."

Then they all disappear through the window. In his sleep, Anton hears the silver-clear tinkle of the little bell:

Klingelingeling, klingelingeling, klingelingeling.

The tinkle grows quieter and quieter until it finally disappears. The only sound to be heard is the gentle breathing of the little goatherd.